Before

illustrated by
JING JING TSONG

written by
LAURA KRAUSS MELMED

Met

Beach Lane Books • New York London Toronto Sydney New Dehli

Before we met,
I kept you safe
where you were meant to be.

Before we met,
I dreamt your smile
was shining back at me.

Before we met,
I dreamt your skin
was softer than a flower.

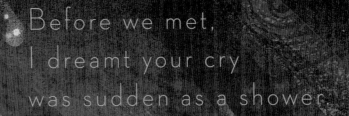

Before we met,
I dreamt your cry
was sudden as a shower.

Before we met,
I dreamt my arms
would rock you like a boat.

Before we met,
I dreamt we danced
to songs a songbird wrote.

Before we met,
I dreamt I felt
the beating of your heart.

Before we met,
I promised you
I'd love you from the start.

And on the day
we met at last . . .

I held you close and knew

the one I had
been dreaming of
was here . . .

and it was you!

Beach Lane Books • An imprint of Simon & Schuster Children's Publishing Division • 1230 Avenue of the Americas, New York, New York 10020 • Text copyright © 2016 by Laura Krauss Melmed • Illustrations copyright © 2016 by Jing Jing Tsong • All rights reserved, including the right of reproduction in whole or in part in any form. • BEACH LANE BOOKS is a trademark of Simon & Schuster, Inc. • For information about special discounts for bulk purchases, please contact Simon & Schuster Special Sales at 1-866-506-1949 or business@simonandschuster.com. • The Simon & Schuster Speakers Bureau can bring authors to your live event. For more information or to book an event, contact the Simon & Schuster Speakers Bureau at 1-866-248-3049 or visit our website at www.simonspeakers.com. • Book design by Lauren Rille. • The text for this book is set in Neutraface. • The illustrations for this book are digitally collaged in Adobe Illustrator. • Manufactured in China • 0216 SCP • First Edition • 10 9 8 7 6 5 4 3 2 1 • Library of Congress Cataloging-in-Publication Data • Melmed, Laura Krauss, author. • Before we met / Laura Krauss Melmed ; illustrated by Jing Jing Tsong.—First edition. • p. cm. • Summary: In simple, rhyming text, a mother expresses her love to her unborn child.
ISBN 978-1-4424-4156-9 (hardcover)
ISBN 978-1-4424-4157-6 (eBook)
1. Mother and child—Juvenile fiction. 2. Stories in rhyme. [1. Stories in rhyme.
2. Mother and child—Fiction. 3. Love—Fiction.] I. Tsong, Jing Jing, illustrator. II. Title.
PZ8.3.M55155Be 2016
[E]—dc23
2014043642

For Devash Tao,
the one his mommy waited for
—L. K. M.

For Tien and Reid
—J. J. T.